MAD for MATH

NAVIGATE THE HIGH SEAS!

EDITED BY LINDA BERTOLA

ILLUSTRATIONS BY AGNESE BARUZZI

Dragon Fruit

WSKids
WHITE STAR KIDS

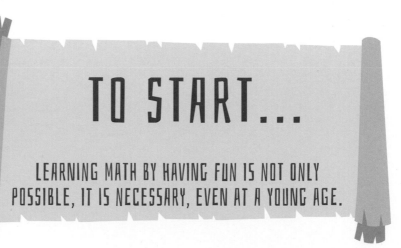

TO START...

LEARNING MATH BY HAVING FUN IS NOT ONLY POSSIBLE, IT IS NECESSARY, EVEN AT A YOUNG AGE.

This book offers activities and chances to approach the world of numbers in a captivating, motivating way that also facilitates a positive attitude towards math.

Pedagogical studies have shown how the motivation at the base of long-lasting learning is linked to enjoyment: this is why we have chosen a playful approach.

Playing fosters intuition and the acquisition of fundamental mathematical concepts. The distinctive setting and the guide-characters leading the child reinforce positive participation. Each chapter begins with a short story that links the mathematical tasks to a "reality," even if it is an imaginary one. Moreover, this narrative approach stimulates children's curiosity.

Topics are presented in a gradual, intuitive way. We have chosen an inductive approach, therefore concepts are never formalized; we have not given any definitions or used specific terminology. We have also proposed some easy "do-it-yourself" ideas that can be made with common materials (or with something included in the book) in order to foster learning through a creative-tactile approach.

THIS BOOK IS AIMED AT CHILDREN IN GRADE 4 TO 5.

CONTENT:

- Operations with decimal numbers

- Fractions

- Percentages

- Reasoning

SOME ADVICE FOR THE ADULTS:

Respect children's timing and their "refusals"! If they close the book or skip a page, it doesn't mean they are giving up. Maybe they just need to quietly process their thinking.

Ask questions, don't give answers! If your child asks for help, don't tell him or her the answer. Ask targeted questions to help them understand the task or the mistake they made.

Let children find their own way, even if it's a long, twisted one. You could then help them explore other roads and maybe find the more clever one to reach the solution.

The first step is solving and understanding. Help children elaborate their thoughts, by asking them to explain verbally or by drawing or using tangible materials in the proposed setting before trying to find a solution or calculation: that's the easiest and least fun part!

Ask "how did you do that?" Gradually get them used to explaining their reasoning: knowing how I reflected and why is much more important than the name of the rule I applied.

The settings proposed in this book are obviously born from our imagination. You can help children retrace numbers and math in their daily lives. Get out of the book and meet math!

ALL ABOARD!

This is a pirate story, and like in all pirate stories worthy of this name, there is a captain and his loyal crew, a ship, several cannonballs, a treasure island, a parrot and hundreds of... potatoes. But let's start from the beginning, I'm Rico, the ship's parrot, I speak little but I hear everything, and I open my mouth to help my pirate friends when they need me. Come with me, I'll introduce them to you.

CAPTAIN POTATO is the name of our captain. You're probably wondering why such a valiant pirate has such a funny name. Well, it's very simple: everybody has used this nickname, ever since he was a young ship's boy, both for the shape of his nose (which looks a bit like a spud) and because the captain has always had a strong passion for... mashed potatoes!

Our travel mates are CURLYBEARD, SKINNYLEG AND ALLROUND.

Curlybeard - I don't think I need to explain why he's called this – knows all the waves in the sea, very wise but a bit hard of hearing. Skinnyleg and Allround are twins, but they have nothing in common. Skinnyleg is terrified of spiders: there's no cannonball, crocodile or storm that can scare him, but if he sees even the tiniest spider he dashes away, screaming his lungs out. Allround, instead, is able to correctly predict when a storm is about to come when his nose starts itching and he can't help sneezing.

SO THIS IS MY CREW AND, AS YOU MIGHT HAVE GUESSED, IT'S IMPOSSIBLE TO GET BORED WITH THESE PIRATES!

SKINNYLEG   ALLROUND   CAPTAIN POTATO   CURLYBEARD   RICO

READ CAREFULLY AND COLOR IN THE REST OF THE CREW'S CLOTHES.

THE SHIRTS OF THE SHIP'S BOY AND THE BOATSWAIN ARE OF THE SAME COLOR.

THERE'S A BLUE HEADSCARF BETWEEN TO RED ONES.

THE BOATSWAIN HAS A GREEN HEADSCARF.

THE SHIP'S BOY'S SHIRT IS THE SAME COLOR AS THE HELMSMAN'S HEADSCARF.

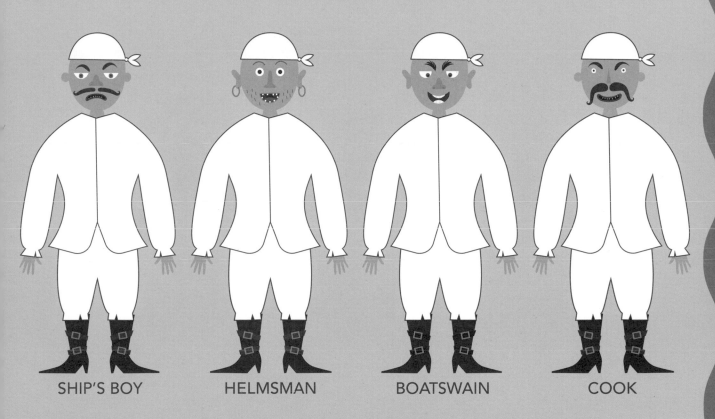

| SHIP'S BOY | HELMSMAN | BOATSWAIN | COOK |

TWO PIRATES ARE WEARING YELLOW PANTS AND ARE AT THE SIDES OF THE LINE.

ONE PIRATE IS WEARING A SHIRT AND A HEADSCARF IN THE SAME COLOR.

NEXT TO A PIRATE WITH YELLOW PANTS THERE IS A PIRATE WITH A YELLOW SHIRT AND A BLUE HEADSCARF.

ONE PIRATE IS WEARING BLACK PANTS.

THE PIRATE WEARING GREEN PANTS DOESN'T HAVE A BLUE HEADSCARF.

CAPTAIN POTATO HAS ORDERED SKINNYLEG AND CURLYBEARD TO RUN SOME ERRANDS BEFORE SAILING OUT!

UNFORTUNATELY, THOUGH, THE TWO PIRATES WEREN'T LISTENING WHEN HE TOLD THEM HOW TO GET TO THE SHOPS.

SOLVE THESE RIDDLES TO HELP THEM. LOOK FOR THE SIGNS AMONG THE STICKERS AT THE END OF THE BOOK AND PUT THEM ON THE SHOPS WITH THE CORRECT NUMBER.

TAILOR'S SHOP: 13 TIMES THE WINGS OF A PELICAN

SMITH'S SHOP: 9 TIMES THE NUMBER OF THE CARDINAL POINTS

MILLER'S SHOP: FOUR TIMES 8 PLUS THREE TIMES 2

CARPENTER'S SHOP: 50 MINUS THE DAYS IN THREE WEEKS

GROCER'S SHOP: THE FEET OF 16 PARROTS MINUS THE EARS OF 7 PIRATES

CAPTAIN POTATO'S CREW HAS TRAVELED TOGETHER FOR YEARS.

THEY'VE HAD SO MANY ADVENTURES TOGETHER! LAUGHTER, FIGHTS, STARRY NIGHTS, FLAT AND ROUGH SEAS... YOU CAN READ THEM ALL IN THE CAPTAIN'S LOG. DECODE IT BY USING THE KEY.

♥ = 1000 ♠ = 1 ♦ = 100 ♣ = 10

SAILS RAISED

♦ ♦ ♥ ♠ ♠ ♠ ♣ ♣ ♣ ♣

STORMS CROSSED

♣ ♣ ♣ ♦ ♦ ♦ ♥ ♥ ♥ ♠ ♠ ♠ ♠ ♠

BARRELS OF JAM

♦ ♥ ♣ ♣ ♦ ♥ ♥ ♠ ♠ ♦ ♦ ♣

APPLE PIES

♦ ♠ ♣ ♣ ♣ ♦ ♥ ♣ ♠ ♣ ♥

CAREFUL! THE CODE HAS CHANGED!

⭐ = 5000

✸ = 500

▲ = 50

🌙 = 5

🌀 = 1

CANNONBALLS SHOT ....

BATTLES WITH OTHER PIRATES ....

CINNAMON BUNS ....

ISLANDS EXPLORED ....

CROCODILES ENCOUNTERED ....

CIDER PINTS ....

POTATOES PEELED ....

THE CREW IS ALMOST READY TO GO!

THEY JUST NEED TO LOAD THE CARGO, BUT BE CAREFUL! IN ORDER TO KEEP THE SHIP BALANCED, THE CRATES NEED TO BE LOADED IN TWO GROUPS: ONE AT THE STERN AND ANOTHER AT THE BOW. EACH GROUP MUST HAVE THE SAME NUMBER OF CRATES AND WEIGH THE SAME. TO LOAD THE SHIP, LOOK FOR THE CRATES AMONG THE STICKERS AT THE END OF THE BOOK.

THE THEFT

"You call this mashed potatoes?" is what Captain Potato usually says when something is not done properly. He's such a mashed-potato expert that he firmly believes they are not all the same. Not all mashed potatoes are made properly and absolutely none can ever compare to the ones his Grandma Gina makes, the ones she has spoiled her grandson with ever since he was a baby.

You must know that many years ago, before leaving for a long trip that would have kept him far from his beloved grandma and her mashed potatoes for a very long time, Captain Potato was gifted with something truly invaluable: the ladle the nice old lady had used for years. This is Captain Potato's most prized treasure.

Well, you can imagine his shock when this morning, the captain went down to the pantry to have breakfast and couldn't find his precious tool. All activities were immediately stopped and all travels put off. The whole crew engaged in a careful but equally useless ladle hunt. The whole ship was combed thoroughly, but to no avail: there was no trace of the missing ladle.

Captain Potato has been weeping since this morning, but his crew got off the ship to keep on searching and catch the ladle thief. In the intricate alleys leading to the harbor, Curlybeard, who is hard of hearing but has an incredible nose, found some traces of delicious mashed potatoes. The pirates immediately start following the tracks and solving the mystery seems closer and closer when...

AAAAAATTCHOOOOOO!

Allround's unmistakable sneeze signals a storm is coming. In less than no time, the sky covers up and rain starts to fall, washing away the traces of mashed potatoes that could have led the pirates to the ladle thief.

In the end, after searching a bit more, the pirates find out the thief and his loot are hiding in a castle, but getting the ladle back won't be easy...

COMPLETE THE PATH WITH THE SYMBOLS BELOW.

THE PLANKS CAN BE PUT NEAR EACH OTHER IF THEY HAVE THE SAME SYMBOL, AND ALL SYMBOLS MUST APPEAR THE SAME NUMBER OF TIMES (INCLUDING THE ONES THE PIRATES HAVE ALREADY PUT). USE THE STICKERS YOU'LL FIND AT THE END OF THE BOOK!

THE PIRATES ARE CHASING THE LADLE THIEF!

HELP THEM FOLLOW HIS TRACES. LINK THE SPOTS OF MASHED POTATOES TOGETHER IN DESCENDING ORDER TO FOLLOW THE TRACK.

THE LADLE HAS BEEN HIDDEN ON ONE OF THESE FOUR ISLANDS.

TO FIND THE RIGHT ONE, AT EVERY JUNCTION, TAKE THE ROAD
WITH THE HIGHEST NUMBER.

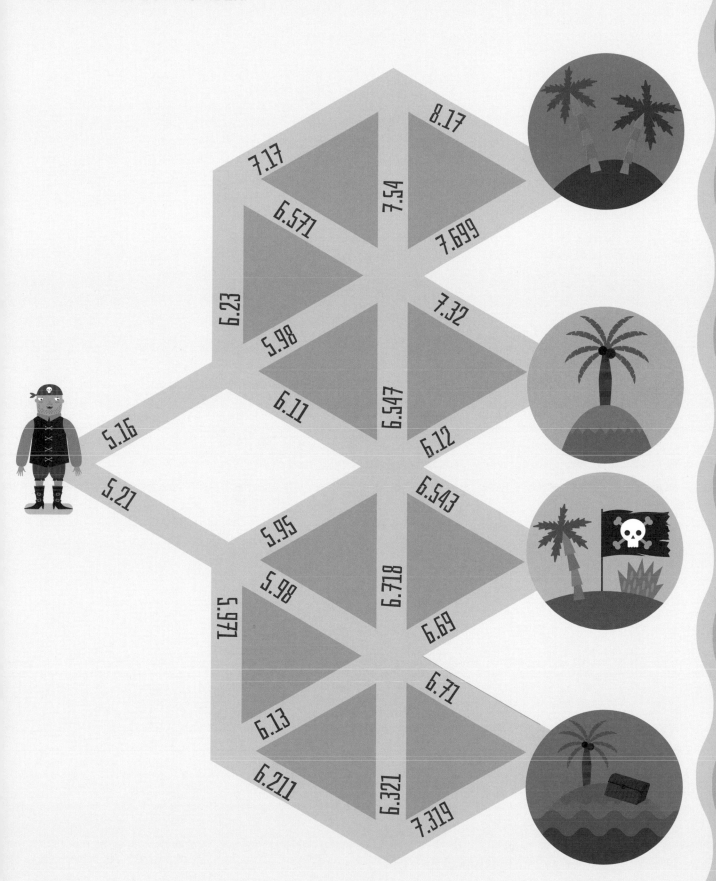

WHEN THEY GET ON THE ISLAND, THE FOUR PIRATES BUMP INTO A FORTIFIED CASTLE.

MAYBE THE LADLE'S IN THERE? HOW CAN THEY GET INSIDE? LUCKILY, RICO HAS ALREADY FIGURED IT OUT! READ WHAT HE SUGGESTS TO MAKE THE DOOR OPEN.

FOLLOW THE DIRECTION OF THE ARROWS TO FILL IN THE GRID USING NUMBERS FROM 0.1 TO 0.9. THE NUMBERS YOU WRITE MUST ADD UP TO THE NUMBER ON THE ARROW, AND YOU CAN'T USE THE SAME NUMBER TWICE WITHIN AN ARROW'S PATH.

		1.1 ↓	0.4 ↓	
	1.7 ↓			0.3 ←
0.6 ↓		0.8		2 ←
	0.3		0.6 ←	
		0.9 ←		

UNBELIEVABLE!

WHEN THE PIRATES MANAGE TO GET IN, AND THEY FIND PIRATE BLACKHAWK'S LOOT... EVERYWHERE! THERE ARE LADLES HANGING FROM THE WALLS AND SCATTERED AROUND THE FLOOR—EVEN A PILE OF WOODEN LADLES! PIRATES USUALLY LOOK FOR GOLDEN COINS, AND THEY SOMETIMES STEAL VESSELS, BUT NEVER KITCHENWARE!

THE LADLE BELONGING TO CAPTAIN POTATO'S GRANDMOTHER HAS BEEN GIVEN THE NUMBER 7. WORK OUT THE RULE AND COMPLETE THE NUMBERS, THEN DO THE CALCULATIONS TO FIND IT.

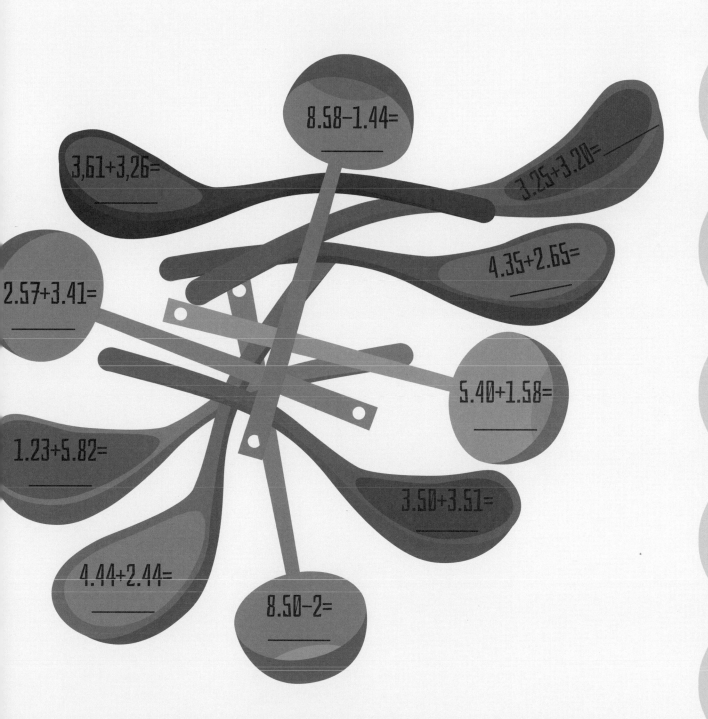

8.58−1.44=
_____

3,61+3,26=
_____

3.25+3.20= _____

2.57+3.41=
_____

4.35+2.65=
_____

5.40+1.58=
_____

1.23+5.82=
_____

3.50+3.51=
_____

4.44+2.44=
_____

8.50−2=
_____

PIRATES AT THE AMUSEMENT PARK

There's something Captain Potato's crew can't really do without.

IS IT PLUNDERING TREASURES? FIGHTING AT SEA UNTIL THE LAST CANNON-BALL IS SHOT? DODGING CROCODILES? NO, NOTHING LIKE THAT.

The captain and his pirates love going to the amusement park. Yes, you heard right! Little flags and sparkly lights, the music of the ice-cream cart, piles of popcorn... there's nothing better than this for Captain Potato and his crew, except, of course, a plate of piping hot mashed potatoes.

Each time the pirates go back to dry land after a long voyage at sea, the amusement park is a must-go for them. Allround loves the Ferris wheel, he goes on it first thing in the morning and gets off when the sun is setting. Skinnyleg doesn't like the Ferris wheel: crouching on that little seat really bothers his long legs. He prefers playing darts. A steady hand, concentration, precision and thud... his aim is not always perfect but having fun is always a guarantee.

Curlybeard and Captain Potato favor sweets to games. If you go to the amusement park you can be sure to find them near the sweets stand: one with a bucket full of hot, fragrant popcorn, the other dealing with a white, sticky cloud of cotton candy.

EACH PIRATE CAN THROW THREE TIMES.

PUT THE MISSING DARTS ON THE TARGET.

43
POINTS

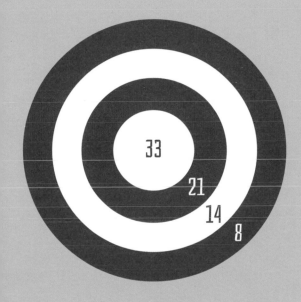

50
POINTS

55
POINTS

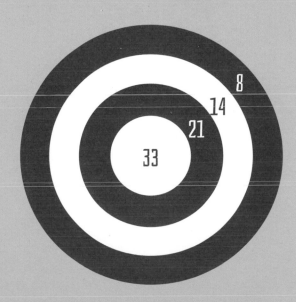

THE CAN TOSS CHALLENGE.

BY MAKING ALL THE CANS FALL, EACH PIRATE WOULD GET 15 POINTS.
FIND OUT WHAT SCORE THEY GOT BY ADDING THE NUMBERS ON THE FALLEN
CANS. BUT BE CAREFUL: IN TWO CASES YOU CAN'T READ THE NUMBERS BECAUSE
THE CANS ARE THE OTHER WAY AROUND... HOW CAN YOU CALCULATE IT?

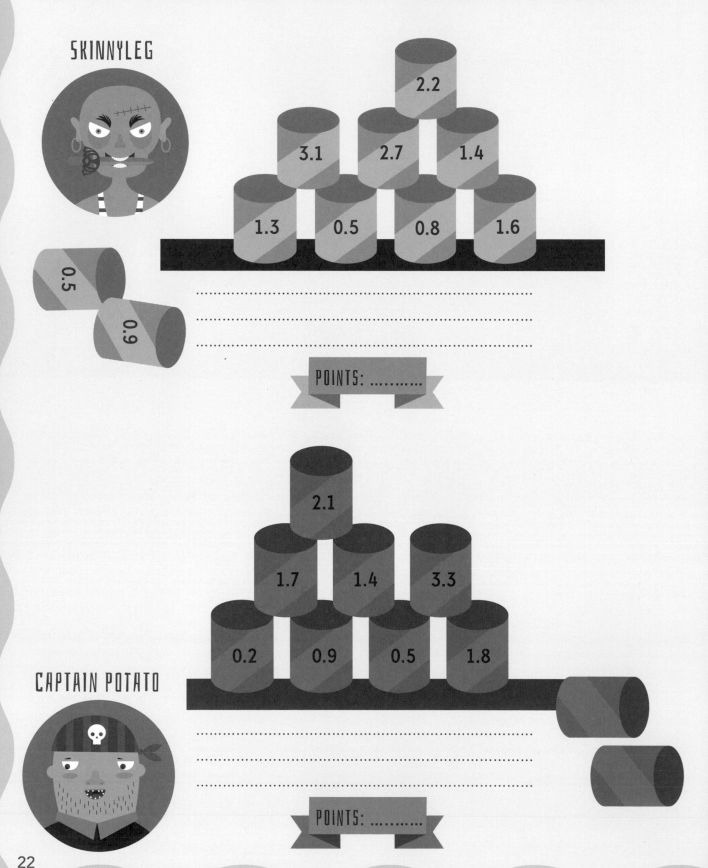

SKINNYLEG

POINTS: ....

CAPTAIN POTATO

POINTS: ....

22

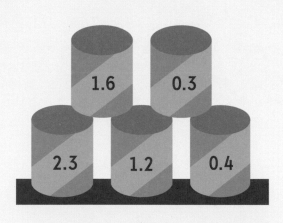

1.6 0.3
2.3 1.2 0.4
1.7 3.1 1.1
2.6 0.7

CURLYBEARD

....
....
....

POINTS: ....

1.9
2.8 0.4
0.8 2.7 3.2

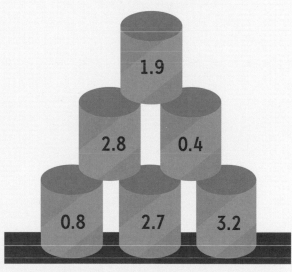

ALLROUND

....
....
....

POINTS: ....

AFTER PLAYING, IT'S SNACK TIME FOR THE FOUR PIRATES.
READ THE PRICES AND HELP THEM CALCULATE.

I'D LIKE A DOUGHNUT, A LOLLIPOP AND SOME LEMONADE.
BUT I DON'T KNOW IF I HAVE ENOUGH MONEY!

....
....
....

CAPTAIN POTATO

I'D LIKE SOME COTTON CANDY AND A LOLLIPOP.
WHAT DRINK CAN I BUY WITH THE MONEY I HAVE LEFT?

....
....
....

2 2 1

SKINNYLEG

I'D LIKE A BAG OF POPCORN, 2 DOUGHNUTS AND
AN ORANGE SODA. HOW MUCH CHANGE WILL I GET?

....
....
....

2 2 1

CURLYBEARD

THE PIRATES ARE PLAYING BINGO.

DO THE CALCULATIONS AND COVER THE RESULTS ON THE CARDS TO FIND OUT WHO WINS.

1) $6.2-2.2=$
2) $7.5 \times 2+1=$
3) $13.8+9.2=$
4) $7.5-3.8-2.7=$
5) $1.2 \times 3 \times 10-1=$
6) $0.5 \times 4=$
7) $5.2 \times 4+4.2=$
8) $17.7+29.3=$
9) $1.5 \times 2 \times 3=$
10) $2.5 \times 2 \times 3+3=$

CAPTAIN POTATO

4	12	35
28	16	47

SKINNYLEG

23	35	42
1	12	29

ALLROUND

2	25	18
47	16	23

CURLYBEARD

36	47	15
25	4	23

THE WINNER IS

....

PROBLEMS AT THE AMUSEMENT PARK

A JAR CONTAINS 9 MARBLES. 4 ARE RED, 3 ARE YELLOW AND 2 ARE GREEN. HOW MANY MARBLES WILL A BLINDFOLDED SKINNYLEG NEED TO PICK UP SO THAT HE CAN BE SURE HE HAS TWO OF THE SAME COLOR IN HIS HAND?

100 GRAMS OF PEANUTS EQUAL 1 HECTOGRAM OF PEANUTS. 10 HECTOGRAMS EQUAL ONE KILO. ALLROUND HAS BOUGHT 2 KILOS AND A HALF OF PEANUTS. HOW MANY GRAMS ARE THEY?

CURLYBEARD IS WAITING FOR HIS TURN TO GO ON THE FERRIS WHEEL. EACH RIDE IS 3 MINUTES AND 20 SECONDS LONG. THE LAST RIDE DEPARTED 90 SECONDS AGO. HOW LONG IS LEFT UNTIL THE NEXT RIDE?

3

CAPTAIN POTATO HAS BOUGHT SOME LOTTERY TICKETS. IF 1,995 TICKETS HAVE BEEN SOLD OVERALL, IS IT MORE LIKELY FOR A 3-DIGIT OR A 4-DIGIT NUMBER TO BE DRAWN?

4

TROUBLE AHEAD!

After years of incursions on the seven seas, hundreds of battles, dozens of treasures looked for (and none found), Captain Potato has made a historic decision. Never had a captain dared so much, no pirate before him had ever even thought about such a thing.

CAPTAIN POTATO AND HIS CREW HAVE BOOKED A HOLIDAY!

They are going on a cruise tomorrow: five days with no sails to furl, decks to polish or mashed potatoes to stir. The luggage is ready, the pirates are as smartly dressed as ever: they are flaunting shirts with no holes and new headscarves for this occasion. They have even showered and combed their hair, beards and mustaches.

Everything's ready, but just when the pirates are about to leave their vessel to go on a modern cruise ship... *BOOOM!*

"For potatoes' sake! What was that?" Captain Potato asks, astonished.
"It's surely not a thunderstorm, I haven't sneezed!" Allround states.
"Did somebody say something? I think I've heard a noise, but I'm not sure..." Curlybeard wonders.
"You're asking if we heard anything? For ladles' sake! You really are as deaf as a doorpost."
"Captain, there's a problem!" Skinnyleg cries out after inspecting the horizon with his spyglass. "They're attacking us!"

That's right, a pirate can never relax when he's at sea, never mind thinking about going on holiday! Their suitcases are soon unpacked, the pirates are at their battle posts in less than a minute, and three ships appear on the horizon... but who are they?

THE SHIP IS (OR BETTER, WAS) READY TO SET SAIL ON A QUIET AND RELAXING CRUISE.

HOW MANY TRIANGLES CAN YOU SEE IN THE SAIL?

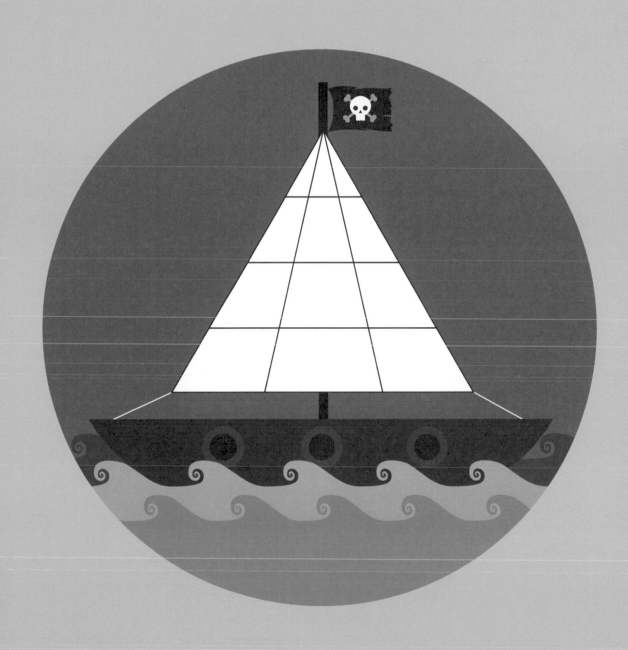

CAPTAIN POTATO AND HIS CREW ARE ABOUT TO MEET THEIR ENEMIES!

BUT THEY DON'T KNOW WHO THEY'RE GOING TO FACE YET. READ THE CLUES AND, HELPING YOURSELF WITH THE GRIDS, FIND OUT THE DIFFERENT COMBINATIONS. (PUT A + WHEN THE INFORMATION IS DEFINITELY TRUE, AND A – WHEN YOU'RE SURE IT'S FALSE.)

FIND OUT HOW MANY PIRATES THERE ARE IN EACH CREW FIGHTING AGAINST CAPTAIN POTATO.

	13 PIRATES	9 PIRATES	12 PIRATES	14 PIRATES
CAPTAIN BREAKBONES	–	+	–	–
CAPTAIN HARDHEAD		–		
CAPTAIN BLACKEYE		–		
CAPTAIN CROOKEDTOOTH		–		

1) CAPTAIN BREAKBONES HAS LESS THAN A DOZEN PIRATES IN HIS CREW.

2) CAPTAIN HARDHEAD HAS LESS PIRATES THAN CROOKEDTOOTH.

3) ON BLACKEYE'S SHIP, THERE'S AN EVEN NUMBER OF PIRATES.

4) BREAKBONES' CREW HAS AT LEAST 3 PIRATES LESS THAN BLACKEYE'S.

PIRATE	CREW
....	....
....	....
....	....
....	....

THOSE FOUR FEARSOME PIRATES LIVE ON FOUR FRIGHTFUL ISLANDS.

CAPTAIN POTATO MUST FACE THEM, BUT THEY ARE PROTECTED BY FOUR TERRIBLE TRAPS. FIND OUT WHICH.

	SKULL ISLAND	STORMY ISLAND	CURSED ISLAND	NAMELESS ISLAND	VOLCANO	CROCODILES	MAZE	CARNIVOROUS PLANTS
CAPTAIN BREAKBONES								
CAPTAIN HARDHEAD								
CAPTAIN BLACKEYE								
CAPTAIN CROOKEDTOOTH								
VOLCANO								
CROCODILES								
MAZE								
CARNIVOROUS PLANTS								

MATCHES

CAPTAIN BREAKBONES

....

CAPTAIN HARDHEAD

....

CAPTAIN BLACKEYE

....

CAPTAIN CROOKEDTOOTH

....

CLUES:

1. THERE'S A MAZE ON SKULL ISLAND.
2. CROOKEDTOOTH DOES NOT LIVE ON STORMY ISLAND, NOR ARE THERE ANY CROCODILES THERE.
3. NAMELESS ISLAND IS NOT FULL OF CROCODILES, AND IT'S NOT BLACKEYE'S ISLAND.
4. CAPTAIN BLACKEYE LIVES IN A FOREST FULL OF CARNIVOROUS PLANTS.
5. NEITHER BREAKBONES NOR BLACKEYE LIVE ON SKULL ISLAND.
6. NEITHER HARDHEAD NOR BLACKEYE LIVE ON CURSED ISLAND.
7. THE VOLCANO IS ON HARDHEAD'S ISLAND.

THE FIRST BATTLE IS AGAINST BREAKBONES' CREW.

AFTER THE FIGHT, CAPTAIN POTATO IS DOING A STOCK INVENTORY. HELP HIM FILL IT IN BY WRITING THE PERCENTAGE OF THE THINGS HE'S GOT LEFT (THE COLORED PART), OR BY COMPLETING THE DIAGRAM.

CANNONBALLS

$$\frac{37}{100} = 37\%$$

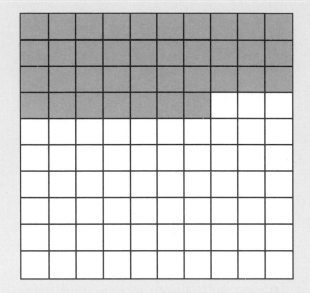

BARRELS OF CIDER
(FIGHTING MAKES US THIRSTY)

$$\frac{}{100} = \ldots\ldots\%$$

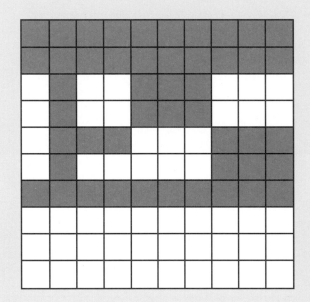

GOOSE FEATHERS
(TICKLING IS A TERRIBLE WEAPON)

$$\frac{53}{100} = \ldots\ldots\%$$

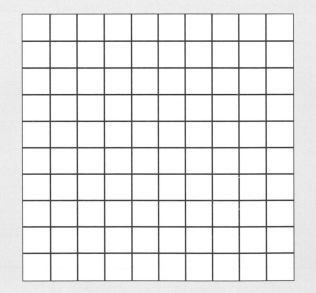

POTATOES
(WE CAN FIGHT BETTER IF OUR BELLIES
ARE FULL OF MASHED POTATOES)

―― =......%

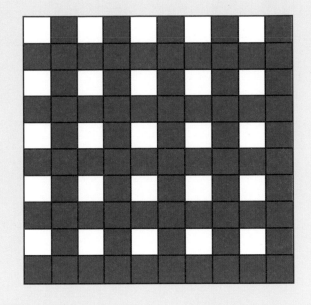

PEPPER GRAINS
(TO MAKE OUR ENEMIES SNEEZE)

―― =63%

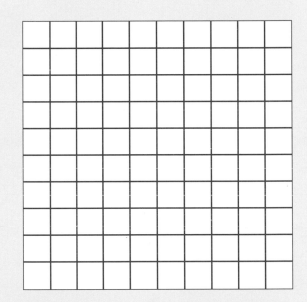

BAGS OF FLOUR
(TO CREATE A CLOUD AND... RUN AWAY!)

―― =......%

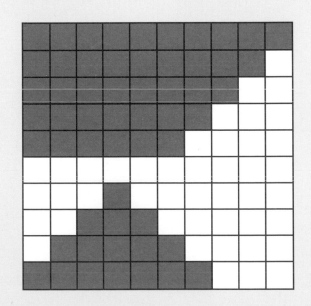

ONE FIGHT DOWN, BUT HERE'S ANOTHER ONE!

THE FIGHT AGAINST THE FEARSOME CAPTAIN HARDHEAD IS ABOUT TO START. MATCH EACH BALL TO THE CANNON IT WAS SHOT FROM. YOU'LL RECOGNIZE THEM BECAUSE THEY HAVE AN EQUAL VALUE. (HERE'S A TIP: FOLLOW THE INSTRUCTIONS TO COLOR THE BALL AND IT WILL BE EASIER TO SPOT THE EQUIVALENCE.)

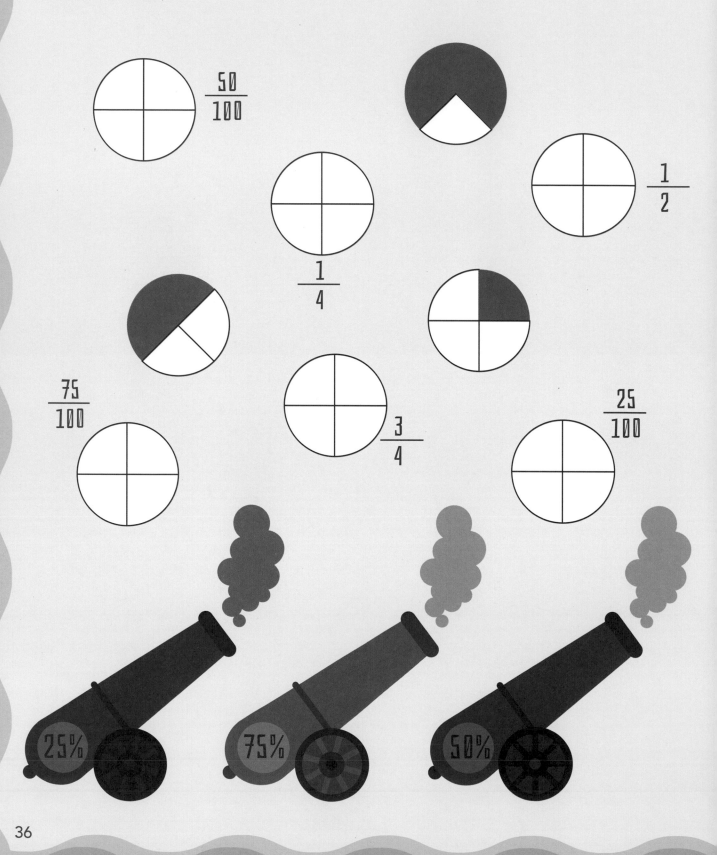

CAPTAIN HARDHEAD REALLY LIVES UP TO HIS NAME!

HE'S NOT GIVING UP AND KEEPS ON FIGHTING, BUT CAPTAIN POTATO HAS A SECRET WEAPON: THE ONION-THROWING SLINGSHOT!

IN A HEARTBEAT, ALL ENEMIES ARE IN TEARS AND LEAVE THE SHIP TO LOOK FOR TISSUES. FIND OUT WHAT ONION WAS THROWN BY EACH PIRATE. LOOK FOR THEM ON THE THE STICKERS PAGE AND STICK THEM IN THE CORRECT SPOTS.

BLACKEYE'S DOMINO.

CAPTAIN POTATO IS RUNNING AWAY FROM BLACKEYE. YOU CAN RETRACE HIS STEPS BY PLAYING DOMINOES. MAKE THE TILES YOURSELF BY USING THE STICKERS AT THE END OF THE BOOK!

PREPARATION
STICK THE STICKERS ON A PIECE OF LIGHT CARDBOARD AND CUT THE TILES.

PLAYERS
FROM 2 TO 4

 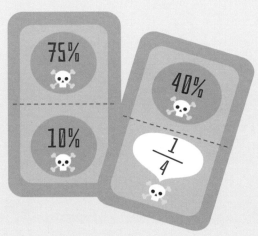

RULES
GIVE 7 TILES TO EACH PLAYER, PUT THE ONES LEFT (THERE WILL BE NONE IF THERE ARE FOUR PLAYERS) FACE DOWN ON THE TABLE.

THE YOUNGER PLAYER STARTS BY PUTTING A TILE FACE UP ON THE TABLE. THEN ITS THE TURN OF THE PLAYER ON THE LEFT, WHO CAN PUT A TILE NEAR THE ONE THAT IS ALREADY ON THE TABLE, IF THEY HAVE ONE WITH THE SAME VALUE (THE VALUES CAN BE EXPRESSED AS PERCENTAGES, FRACTIONS, OR DRAWINGS). IF THEY CAN'T PUT A TILE DOWN, THEY WILL PICK UP A TILE FROM THE ONES THAT ARE FACE DOWN ON THE TABLE. IT'S NOW THE NEXT PLAYER'S TURN. IF THERE ARE NO TILES TO PICK UP, THE TURN PASSES IMMEDIATELY.

THE WINNER IS THE FIRST TO PUT ALL OF THEIR TILES ON THE TABLE.

IF THERE IS A DRAW AND NO ONE CAN PUT TILES DOWN, SUM UP THE TILES EACH PLAYER HAS AND THE WINNER IS THE ONE WITH THE SMALLEST VALUE.

HAVE FUN!

THE LAST FIGHT IS AGAINST CROOKEDTOOTH, AN OLD SEA DOG.

HE ALSO GAVE UP IN THE END, BUT CAPTAIN POTATO WAS FORCED TO USE HIS "ACE IN THE HOLE"... WHICH IS INVITING EVERYBODY ON BOARD FOR A DELICIOUS MASHED-POTATO FEAST. NO PIRATE COULD EVER RESIST SOMETHING LIKE THIS!

AFTER ALL THESE FIGHTS, HOWEVER, THE SHIP IS IN DIRE NEED OF MENDING. HELP THE PIRATES BY FOLLOWING THE INSTRUCTIONS AND COLORING IN.

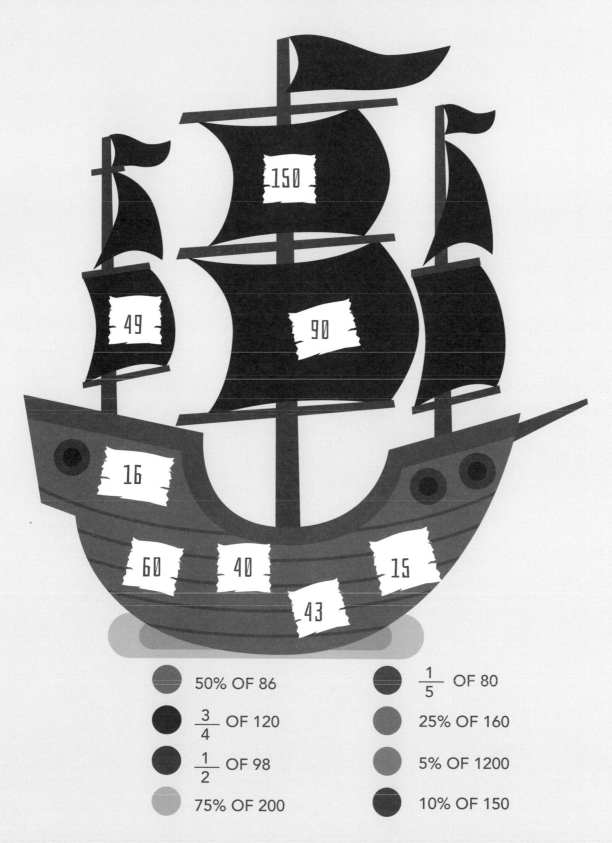

50% OF 86

$\frac{3}{4}$ OF 120

$\frac{1}{2}$ OF 98

75% OF 200

$\frac{1}{5}$ OF 80

25% OF 160

5% OF 1200

10% OF 150

TREASURE HUNTING

How exhausting! After all those battles, Captain Potato and his crew are resting on a little desert island. "Nothing and no one will ever disturb us here," they thought. Curlybeard is happily swimming in the waves, Captain Potato is napping on a hammock under a palm. Skinnyleg and Allround are competing to see who will build the best sandcastle.

BUT AS ALL PIRATES KNOW WELL, THIS IS ONLY THE CALM
BEFORE THE STORM.

And soon enough, all chaos breaks loose: Skinnyleg moves a stone and finds a friendly spider staring at him. He throws his spade in the air and starts running like mad, stepping on Curlybeard's foot, who stumbles and falls on the Captain, making him get tangled in his hammock. And if that wasn't enough, Allround starts sneezing like mad.

WELL THERE'S REALLY NO DOUBT ABOUT IT NOW: QUIETNESS
AND RELAXATION ARE NOT FOR PIRATES!

Luckily there's me, Rico, to save the day with the faded piece of paper I've got furled up in my mouth. Captain Potato unfolds it and reads it carefully: it's a map!

"FINALLY" HE CRIES OUT, "ALL THIS REST WAS DOING NO GOOD FOR US!
LET'S GO... TREASURE HUNTING!"

THE FIRST THING TO DO IS TRY AND DECODE THE MAP.

IT WON'T BE EASY! COMPLETE THESE MAGIC SQUARES: THE NUMBERS IN EACH VERTICAL, HORIZONTAL, AND DIAGONAL ROW MUST ADD UP TO THE VALUE INDICATED BELOW.

2		4
	5	

SUM: 15

8		
	5	
	9	

SUM: 15

1		13	
14	11		7
	5		
15		3	6

SUM: 34

	3		13
	10		
9		7	
4			1

SUM: 34

CAPTAIN POTATO AND HIS CREW HAVE SPOTTED SOMETHING!

THEY'RE NEAR AN ISLAND THAT COULD BE THE ONE HOLDING THE TREASURE. RICO THE PARROT IS FLYING AROUND TO EXAMINE THE AREA. WHEN HE COMES BACK, HE TELLS THE CREW WHAT HE'S FOUND OUT. FOLLOW HIS INSTRUCTIONS AND COLOR THE MAP IN.

- 40% OF THE ISLAND IS COVERED IN FORESTS.
- HALF OF THE REMAINING PART FEATURES LAWNS.
- THERE'S A LAKE AND IT OCCUPIES ONE TENTH OF THE SPACE OCCUPIED BY LAWNS.
- THE REMAINING PART FEATURES BEACHES AND MOUNTAINS. THE MOUNTAINS OCCUPY 10% OF THE AREA OCCUPIED BY FORESTS AND LAWNS.

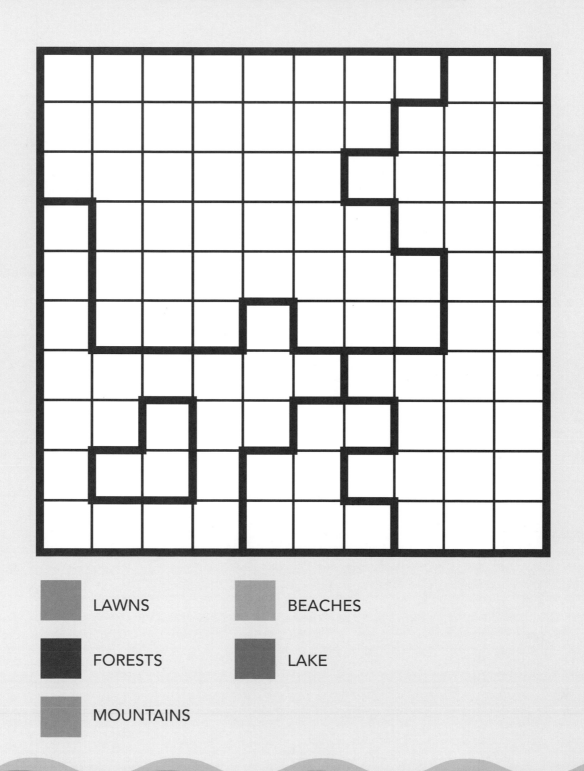

LAWNS

BEACHES

FORESTS

LAKE

MOUNTAINS

WITH HIS SPYGLASS, CAPTAIN POTATO INSPECTS THE ISLAND ON THE HORIZON.

I CAN SEE 17 COCONUTS AND THEY ARE 50% OF THE TOTAL AMOUNT. HOW MANY COCONUTS ARE THERE OVERALL?

I CAN SEE 7 PALMS AND THEY ARE 25% OF THE TOTAL AMOUNT. HOW MANY PALMS ARE THERE OVERALL?

I CAN SEE 12 MONKEYS AND THEY ARE 10% OF THE TOTAL AMOUNT. HOW MANY MONKEYS LIVE ON THE ISLAND?

I CAN SEE 0 TREASURES AND THEY ARE 100% OF THE TOTAL AMOUNT. UNFORTUNATELY THIS IS NOT TREASURE ISLAND, WE MUST KEEP LOOKING!

CAPTAIN POTATO IS STUDYING DIFFERENT MAPS TO DECIDE THE BEST COURSE TO TAKE.

CAN YOU HELP HIM? ON EACH MAP, TRACE THE ROUTE THAT TOUCHES ALL ISLANDS. BE CAREFUL THOUGH, YOU MUST TRACE A CONTINUOUS LINE AND NEVER PASS ON THE SAME TRACK TWICE.

45

AFTER SEVERAL ATTEMPTS, THE PIRATES HAVE FINALLY REACHED TREASURE ISLAND.

THEIR JOURNEY LASTED FROM MAY 13TH TO JUNE 13TH. THE PIRATES HAVE USED 2 BAGS OF FLOUR EVERY 4 DAYS, 2 JARS OF JAM ON ODD DAYS AND 12 BOTTLES OF LEMONADE EVERY 8 DAYS.

HOW MANY SUPPLIES HAVE THEY USED OVERALL?

THE PIRATES HAVE USED 1/3 OF THE TOTAL SUPPLIES. CAN YOU WORK OUT HOW MUCH FLOUR, JAM AND LEMONADE THEY HAD IN THE BEGINNING?

WHEN THEY GO ASHORE, THE PIRATES SOON FIND OUT THE ISLAND IS FULL
OF FRUIT TREES.

THERE ARE BANANA TREES, COCONUT TREES,
AND MANGO TREES. THERE ARE 50 BANANA TREES.
THERE ARE 72% LESS COCONUT TREES THAN
BANANA TREES. THE MANGO TREES ARE 3/8
OF THE NUMBER OF BANANA AND COCONUT
TREES COMBINED.

HOW MANY BANANA, COCONUT
AND MANGO TREES ARE THERE?

THE PATH LEADING TO THE CAVE WHERE THE TREASURE IS HIDDEN IS LINED
WITH PLANTS IN FULL BLOOM. THERE ARE 850 PLANTS OVERALL. 3/5 OF THEM
HAVE GREEN LEAVES, THE REST HAVE YELLOW LEAVES. HALF OF THE PLANTS
WITH YELLOW LEAVES HAVE RED FRUITS, THE OTHER HALF HAVE PURPLE FRUITS.
THE GREEN-LEAFED PLANTS HAVE EITHER ORANGE OR PINK FLOWERS.
THERE ARE 100 LESS PLANTS WITH PINK FLOWERS THAN THOSE WITH ORANGE
FLOWERS.

HOW MANY PLANTS OF EACH KIND ARE THERE?

THE PIRATES ARE FINALLY INSIDE THE CAVE WHERE THE TREASURE IS KEPT.

IN ORDER TO GET IN, THEY MUST ANSWER SOME QUESTIONS FROM AN OLD PELICAN, THE KEEPER OF THIS PLACE. COLOR IN GREEN THE BUBBLES THAT ARE TRUE AND COLOR IN RED THE ONES THAT ARE FALSE.

ALL PIRATES ARE BRAVE
SOME LIONS ARE BRAVE
SOME LIONS ARE PIRATES

ALL TREASURES ARE VALUABLE
FRIENDS ARE TREASURES
THEREFORE, FRIENDS ARE VALUABLE

SOME BIRDS ARE PARROTS
ALL PARROTS HAVE COLORFUL FEATHERS
NOT ALL BIRDS HAVE COLORFUL FEATHERS

ALL PIRATES ARE GOOD
EACH PIRATE IS A SAILOR
ALL SAILORS ARE GOOD

YOU NEED SOME GEMSTONES IN ORDER TO OPEN THE DOOR OF THE TREASURE CHAMBER.

THEY ARE HIDDEN INSIDE A BIG TRUNK THAT CONTAINS 4 SMALLER CHESTS, EACH WITH 3 JEWELRY BOXES INSIDE IT.

IT'S TIME TO PUT THE 5 GEMS ON THIS ROUND PADLOCK. CHOOSE THE GEMS ON THE STICKERS PAGE AND FOLLOW THE INSTRUCTIONS TO STICK THEM IN THE CORRECT PLACE.

THE RED GEM IS NOT NEXT TO THE PURPLE ONE

THE BLUE GEM IS NOT NEXT TO THE PURPLE ONE

THE YELLOW GEM IS NOT TO THE RIGHT OF THE PURPLE ONE

THE RED AND GREEN GEMS ARE NOT NEXT TO EACH OTHER

HURRAY!

THE PIRATES HAVE FINALLY MANAGED TO OPEN THE CHEST AND THE TREASURE IS ALL THEIRS! BUT WHAT WILL IT BE? ANCIENT COINS? JEWELS? DIAMONDS? IT'S ACTUALLY NOTHING LIKE THAT! THE TREASURE IS A BIG, HUGE, ENORMOUS...

BAG OF POTATOES!

ANSWERS

P. 5: COLOR THE PIRATES' CLOTHES IN

SHIP'S BOY   HELMSMAN   BOATSWAIN   COOK

PP. 10-11: THE CARGO LOAD

PP. 6-7: THE PIRATES' ERRANDS

TAYLOR'S SHOP: 26
SMITH'S SHOP: 36
MILLER'S SHOP: 38
CARPENTER'S SHOP: 29
GROCER'S SHOP: 18

PP. 8-9: THE CREW'S ADVENTURES

SAILS RAISED: 1243
STORMS CROSSED: 3435
BARRELS OF JAM: 3532
APPLE PIES: 3242

CANNONBALLS SHOT: 11707
BATTLES WITH OTHER PIRATES: 17166
CINNAMON BUNS: 11278
ISLANDS EXPLORED: 10716
CROCODILES ENCOUNTERED: 7420
CIDER PINTS: 10770
POTATOES PEELED: 5977

PP. 12-13: THE TRAIL

THERE ARE TWO POSSIBLE SOLUTIONS

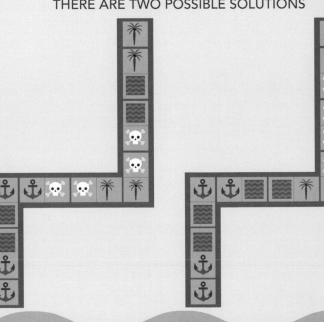

PP. 14–15: FINDING THE LADLE

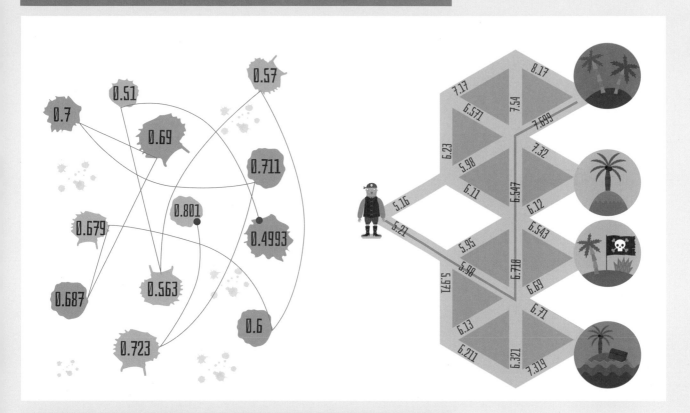

PP. 16–17: THE FORTIFIED CASTLE

	1.2	1.3
1.6	0.7	0.9
0.9	0.5	0.4

	0.5	0.6
0.3	0.2	0.1
0.8	0.3	0.5

		0.1	0.4	
	1.7	0.2	0.1	0.3
0.6	0.9	0.8	0.3	2
0.2	0.3	0.1	0.6	
0.4	0.5	0.9		

PP. 18–19: BLACKHAWK'S LOOT

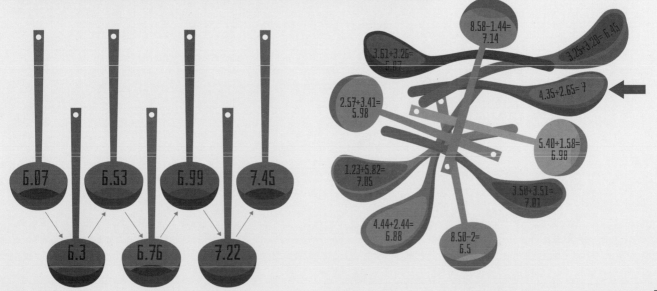

51

P. 21: DARTS

43 POINTS   **50 POINTS**   **55 POINTS**

PP. 22-23: CAN TOSS CHALLENGE

SKINNYLEG: 1.4   CAPTAIN POTATO: 3.1   CURLYBEARD: 9.2   ALLROUND: 3.2

PP. 24-25: THE PIRATES HAVE A SNACK

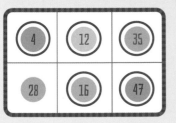   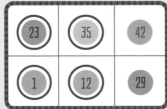   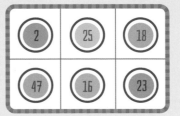

CAPTAIN POTATO:
0.8+0.9+1.8= 3.5
HE HASN'T GOT ENOUGH MONEY!

SKINNYLEG:
2.5+0.9= 3.4
5-3.4= 1.6
HE CAN BUY SOME ORANGE SODA.

CURLYBEARD:
1.7+1.6+0.8+0.8= 4.9
WILL GET 0.1 CHANGE.

PP. 26-27: THE PIRATES PLAY BINGO

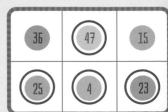

4	12	35
28	16	47

23	35	42
1	12	29

2	25	18
47	16	23

36	47	15
25	4	23

1) 4   2) 16   3) 23   4) 1   5) 35   6) 2   7) 25   8) 47   9) 12   10) 18
WINNER: ALLROUND

1) 4
2) 2500 G
3) 110 SECONDS OR 1 MINUTE AND 50 SECONDS
4) FOUR-DIGIT NUMBERS: 996 TICKETS

PP. 30–31: FIND THE HIDDEN TRIANGLES

24 TRIANGLES

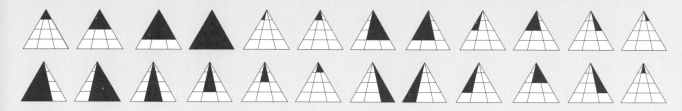

PP. 32–33: FIGHTING THE ENEMIES

	13 PIRATES	9 PIRATES	12 PIRATES	14 PIRATES
CAPTAIN BREAKBONES	−	+	−	−
CAPTAIN HARDHEAD	−	−	+	−
CAPTAIN BLACKEYE	−	−	−	+
CAPTAIN CROOKEDTOOTH	+	−	−	−

PIRATE	CREW
BREAKBONES >	9 PIRATES
HARDHEAD >	12 PIRATES
BLACKEYE >	14 PIRATES
CROOKEDTOOTH >	13 PIRATES

	SKULL ISLAND	STORMY ISLAND	CURSED ISLAND	NAMELESS ISLAND	VOLCANO	CROCODILES	MAZE	CARNIVOROUS PLANTS
CAPTAIN BREAKBONES	−	−	+	−	−	+	−	−
CAPTAIN HARDHEAD	−	−	−	+	+	−	−	−
CAPTAIN BLACKEYE	−	+	−	−				+
CAPTAIN CROOKEDTOOTH	+	−	−	−			+	
VOLCANO	−	−	−	+				
CROCODILES	−	−	+	−				
MAZE	+	−	−	−				
CARNIVOROUS PLANTS	−	+	−	−				

MATCHES

BREAKBONES – CURSED I. – CROCODILES

HARDHEAD – NAMELESS I. – VOLCANO

BLACKEYE – STORMY I. – CARNIVOROUS PLANTS

CROOKEDTOOTH – SKULL I. – MAZE

PP. 34-35: THE PROVISIONS INVENTORY

BARRELS OF CIDER: $\frac{48}{100}$ = 48%   GOOSE FEATHERS: $\frac{53}{100}$ = 53%   POTATOES: $\frac{75}{100}$ = 75%   PEPPER GRAINS: $\frac{63}{100}$ = 63%   FLOUR BAGS: $\frac{56}{100}$ = 56%

PP. 36-37: CANNONBALLS AND ONION THROWS

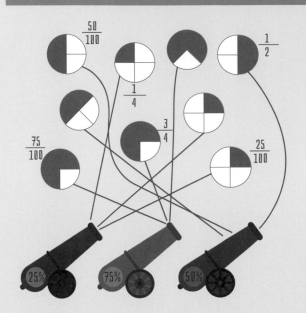

P. 39: LET'S PATCH THE SHIP UP

P. 41: DECODING THE MAP

2	9	4
7	5	3
6	1	8

1	8	13	12
14	11	2	7
4	5	16	9
15	10	3	6

8	1	6
3	5	7
4	9	2

16	3	2	13
5	10	11	8
9	6	7	12
4	15	14	1

PP. 42-43: CAPTAIN POTATO HAS SPOTTED SOMETHING!

1) 17X2 = 34
2) 7X4 = 28
3) 12X10 = 120
4) 0X100 = 0

PP. 44-45: THE ROUTE TO FOLLOW

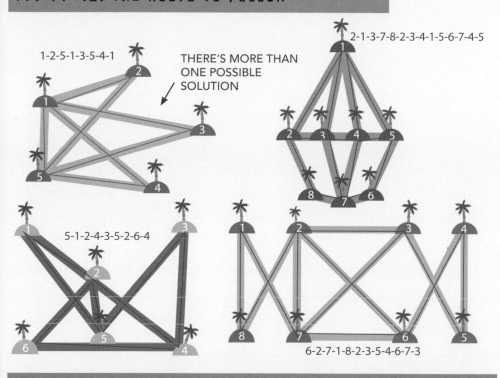

1-2-5-1-3-5-4-1

THERE'S MORE THAN ONE POSSIBLE SOLUTION

2-1-3-7-8-2-3-4-1-5-6-7-4-5

5-1-2-4-3-5-2-6-4

6-2-7-1-8-2-3-5-4-6-7-3

PP. 46-47: THE PIRATES REACH TREASURE ISLAND

IN THE BEGINNING THEY HAD: 24 BAGS OF FLOUR, 51 JARS OF JAM, 72 BOTTLES OF LEMONADE.

1) FROM MAY 13 TO JUNE 13 = 32 DAYS
32:4X2=16

2) 32:8X12= 48

3) THE ODD DAYS ARE 17
13TH ,15TH ,17TH ,19TH ,21ST ,23RD ,25TH ,27TH ,29TH, 31ST MAY
1ST ,3RD ,5TH ,7TH ,9TH ,11TH ,13TH JUNE. 17X2= 34

4) 50 BANANA TREES, 14 COCONUT TREES, 24 MANGO TREES

5) RED: 170, PURPLE: 170, ORANGE: 305, PINK: 205

PP. 48-49: THE TREASURE CAVE

ALL PIRATES ARE BRAVE
SOME LIONS ARE BRAVE
SOME LIONS ARE PIRATES

ALL PIRATES ARE GOOD
EACH PIRATE IS A SAILOR
ALL SAILORS ARE GOOD

ALL TREASURES ARE VALUABLE
FRIENDS ARE TREASURES
THEREFORE, FRIENDS ARE VALUABLE

SOME BIRDS ARE PARROTS
ALL PARROTS HAVE COLORFUL FEATHERS
NOT ALL BIRDS HAVE COLORFUL FEATHERS

THERE'S MORE THAN ONE POSSIBLE SOLUTION

LINDA BERTOLA

A graduate in Foreign Languages for Intercultural Mediation at Milan's Università Cattolica, Linda Bertola is a linguistic and learning facilitator. She focuses on teaching and learning supports for pupils with special educational needs, working both in and out of school. She also specializes in teaching Italian as a foreign language to children, teenagers and adults. She has collaborated with schools and associations as an intercultural teacher. She is passionate about teaching mathematics and making learning fun. She has edited several books for White Star Kids.

AGNESE BARUZZI

Agnese has a degree in Graphic Design from ISIA (Higher Institute for Artistic Industries) in Urbino. Since 2001, she has worked as an illustrator and author: she has made several works for young people in Italy, the United Kingdom, Japan, Portugal, the United States, France and Korea. She carries out workshops for children and adults in schools and libraries, and collaborates with agencies and graphic and editorial studios. In recent years, she has illustrated several titles for White Star Kids.

Copyright © 2022 Linda Bertola. All rights reserved.

Published by DragonFruit, an imprint of Mango Publishing, a division of Mango Publishing Group, Inc.

Mango is an active supporter of authors' rights to free speech and artistic expression in their books. Thank you in advance for respecting our authors' rights. For permission requests, please contact the publisher at:
Mango Publishing Group
2850 Douglas Road, 4th Floor
Coral Gables, FL
33134 USA
info@mango.bz

For special orders, quantity sales, course adoptions and corporate sales, please email the publisher at sales@mango.bz. For trade and wholesale sales, please contact Ingram Publisher Services at customer.service@ingramcontent.com or +1.800.509.4887.

Mad for Math: Navigate the High Seas
ISBN: (p) 978-1-68481-049-9
BISAC: JNF035040, JUVENILE NONFICTION / Mathematics / Fractions

White Star Kids® is a registered trademark property of White Star s.r.l.

© 2019 White Star s.r.l.
Piazzale Luigi Cadorna, 6
20123 Milan, Italy
www.whitestar.it

Translation and Editing: Langue&Parole, Milan (Margaret Greenan)

ISBN 978-88-544-1374-0
1 2 3 4 5 6   23 22 21 20 19

Printed in China

SMITH

TAILOR

CARPENTER

GROCER

MILLER

12 KG

5 KG

3 KG

9 KG

4 KG

7 KG

7 KG

6 KG

2 KG

3 KG

1 KG

1 KG

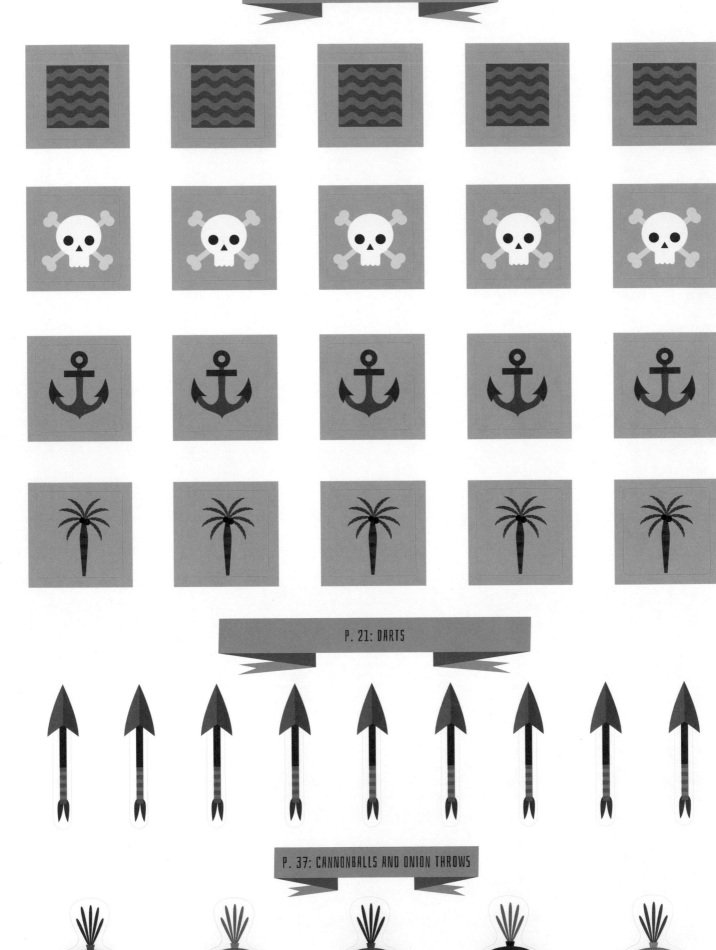

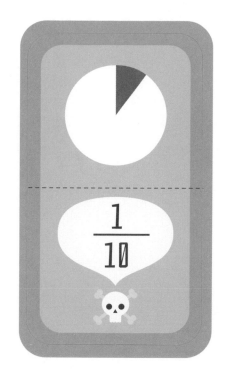

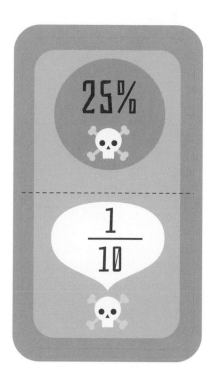

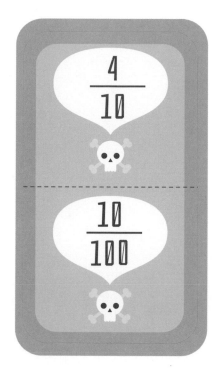

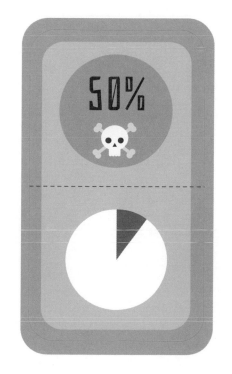

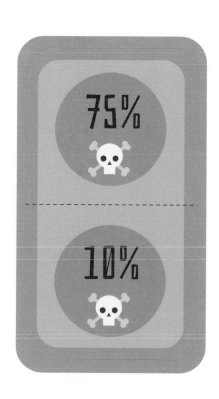

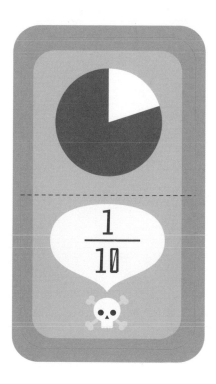

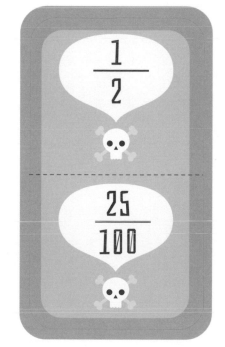

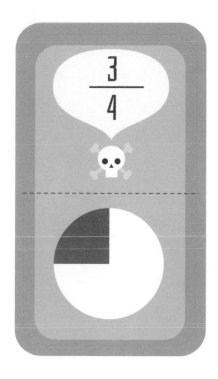

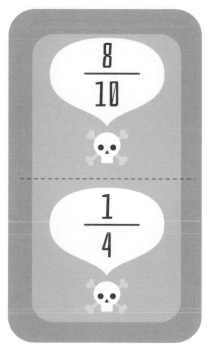

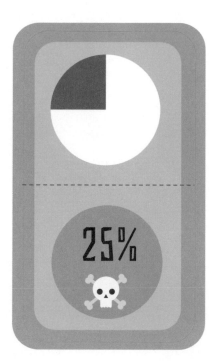

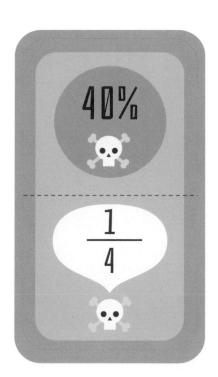

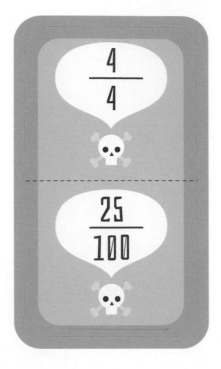

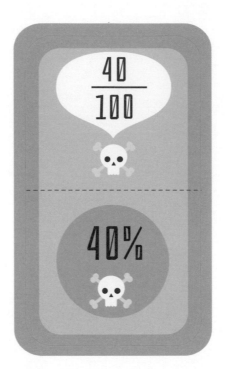

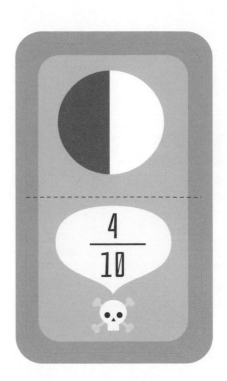

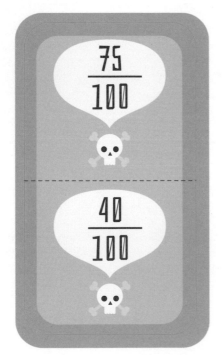

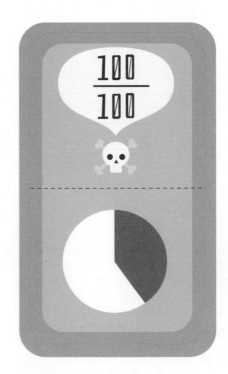

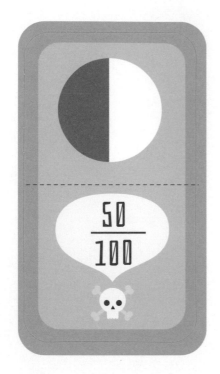

$\dfrac{50}{100}$

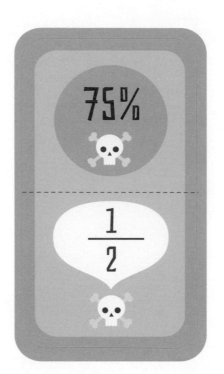
75%

$\dfrac{1}{2}$

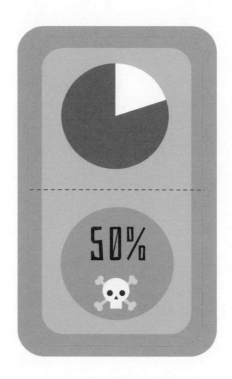

50%

$\dfrac{50}{100}$

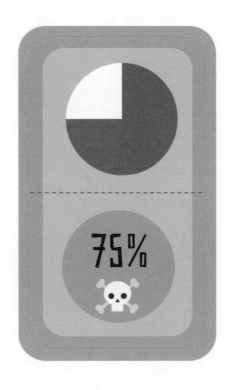

75%

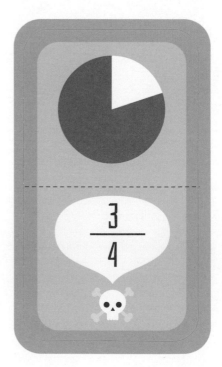

$\dfrac{3}{4}$

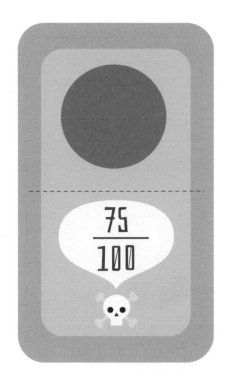

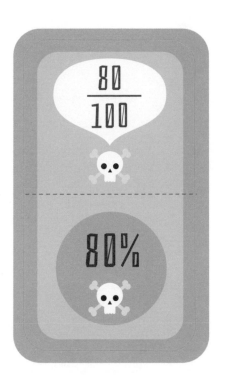

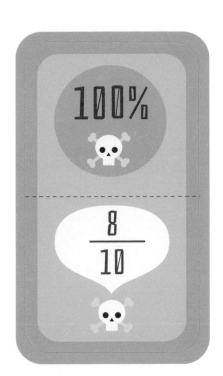

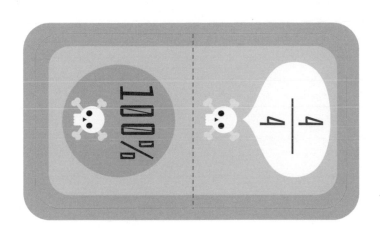

P. 49: THE PADLOCK WITH GEMSTONES

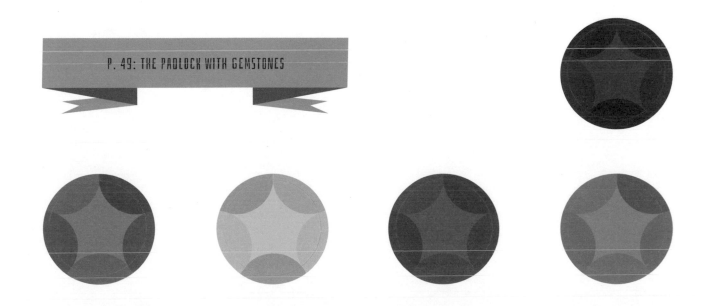

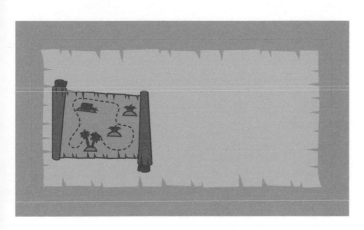

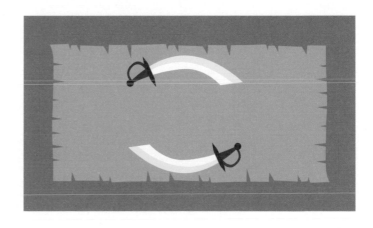